Double Grubby

This story illustrates the value of liking yourself,
because you're better at being you than anyone else.

Story by:
Will Ryan

Illustrated by:
David High
Russell Hicks
Theresa Mazurek
Allyn Conley/Gorniak
Julie Armstrong

W•W
WORLDS OF WONDER ™

Grubby® Newton Gimmick™ Princess Aruzia™ Leota™ Wooly What's-It™

Prince Arin™ Fobs®

It all started one morning when Grubby and I returned to Gimmick's house after a walk.

Page 1

This invention is entirely different.

"I'm Naturally Scientific"

This is the Multiplication Table...the world's first duplicator!

A banana! Oh, heavens to Grundo! Something must be slightly off.

O.K. Gimmick, now try it.

While I helped Gimmick reset the controls, Grubby wandered off.

There are two Grubbys!

The two Grubbys were arguing with each other.

The duplicate Grubby started to go in and out of focus.

"I Like Being Myself"